THE QUAIL'S EGG

A Folk Tale from Sri Lanka

Retold and illustrated by
Joanna Troughton

Blackie
London

Bedrick/Blackie
New York

One day a quail laid an egg.
And then she went to eat some food.

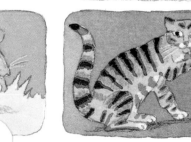

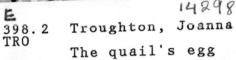

Author's Note

The accumulative tale is a popular way of telling a story throughout the world. The best-known tale of this kind from Britain is the story of the old woman, and her pig who wouldn't jump over the style. *The Quail's Egg* comes from Sri Lanka, but it follows the same pattern as the British story and countless others.

Copyright © Joanna Troughton 1988

First published in 1988 by
Blackie and Son Limited,
7 Leicester Place,
London WC2H 7BP

British Library Cataloguing in Publication Data
Troughton, Joanna
   The quail's egg: a folk tale from Sri
Lanka.
   I. Title
   823'.914[J]   PZ7

   ISBN 0-216-92397-2

Designed in London by
Malcolm Smythe

Typeset in Antique Olive by
Dorchester Typesetting Group

Printed in Spain by
Salingraf, S.A.L. - Bilbao

First American edition published in 1988 by
Peter Bedrick Books
125 East 23rd Street
New York NY 10010

Library of Congress Cataloging-in-Publication Data
Troughton, Joanna.
   The quail's egg.
   (Folk takes of the world)
   Summary: Presents a cumulative folk tale about a
mother quail's efforts to recover her egg after it rolls
into the crevice of a rock.
   [1. Folklore—Sri Lanka]   I. Title. II. Series: Folk
tales of the world (New York, N.Y.)
PZ8.1.T74Qu   1988   398.2'4528617'095493 [E] 87–33376
ISBN 0–87226–185–9

When she returned the egg was gone!
It had rolled away into the crevice of a rock,
and the quail could not reach it.

The quail went to see the mason.
'Mason, please come quickly.
Cut the rock and release my egg.'
But the mason said, 'I will not.'

The quail went to see the pig.
'Pig, go and trample the rice field of the mason,
the mason who did not cut the rock
    and release my egg.'

But the pig said, 'I will not.'

The quail went to see the thorny creeper.
'Thorny creeper, go and prick the pig,
the pig who did not trample the rice field
   of the mason,
the mason who did not
   cut the rock and release my egg.'

But the thorny creeper said, 'I will not.'

The quail went to see the fire.
'Fire, go and burn the thorny creeper,
the thorny creeper who did not
    prick the pig,
the pig who did not
    trample the rice field of the mason,
the mason who did not cut the rock
    and release my egg.'

But the fire said, 'I will not.'

The quail went to see the water pool.
'Water pool, go and put out the fire,
the fire who did not burn the thorny creeper,
the thorny creeper who did not prick the pig,
the pig who did not trample the rice field of
   the mason,
the mason who did not
   cut the rock and release my egg.'

But the water pool said, 'I will not.'

The quail went to see the elephant.
'Elephant, go and muddy the water pool,
the water pool who did not put out the fire,
the fire who did not burn the thorny creeper,
the thorny creeper who did not prick the pig,
the pig who did not trample the rice field of
   the mason,
the mason who did not cut the rock
   and release my egg.'

But the elephant said, 'I will not.'

The quail went to see the mouse.
'Mouse, go and run up the leg of the elephant,
the elephant who did not muddy the water pool,
the water pool who did not put out the fire,
the fire who did not burn the thorny creeper,
the thorny creeper who did not prick the pig,
the pig who did not trample the rice field of
    the mason,
the mason who did not cut the rock
    and release my egg.'

But the mouse said, 'I will not.'

The quail went to see the cat.
'Cat, go and catch the mouse,
the mouse who did not run up the leg of the elephant,
the elephant who did not muddy the water pool,
the water pool who did not put out the fire,
the fire who did not burn the thorny creeper,
the thorny creeper who did not prick the pig,
the pig who did not trample the rice field of
    the mason,
the mason who did not cut the rock
    and release my egg.'

And the cat said, 'I will!'
For the world would come to an end
before a cat would leave a mouse alone.

The cat went to catch the mouse.

The mouse ran up the leg of the elephant.

The elephant muddied the water pool.

The water pool started to put out the fire.

The fire went to burn the
thorny creeper.

The thorny creeper pricked the pig.

The pig began to trample the
rice field of the mason.

The mason cut the rock.
And the quail's egg was free!